The Worry Warthog

Lucy Pickett

Deep in the heart of Africa lived a family of warthogs.

They were gruff...

they were tough...

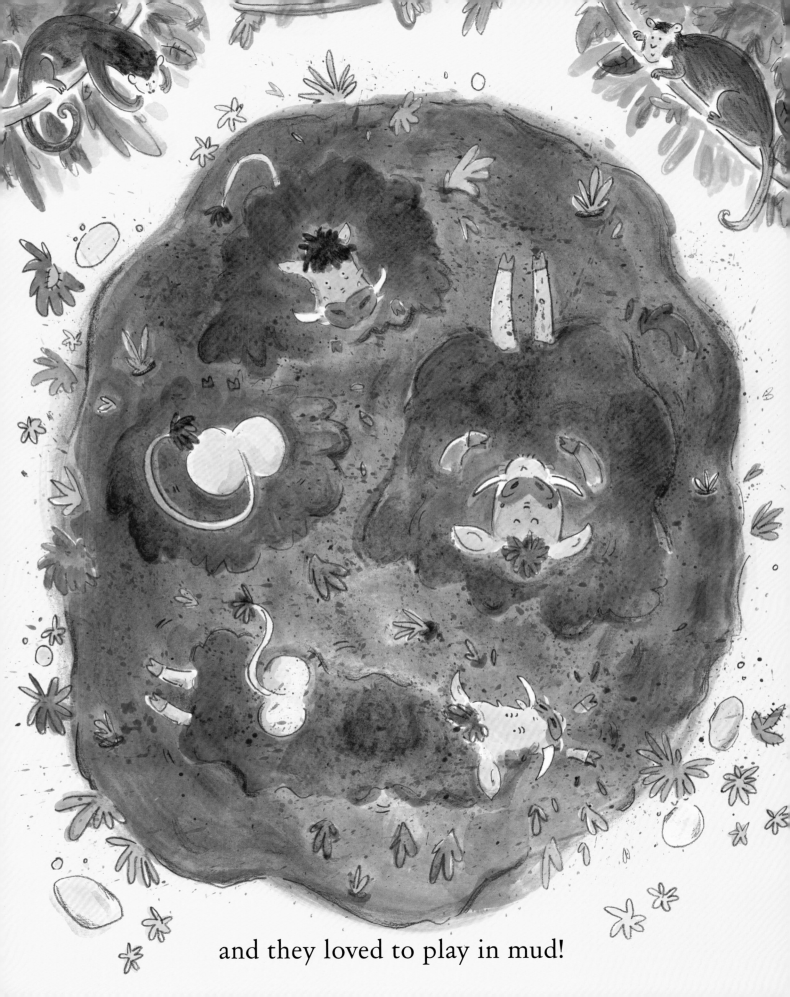

and they loved to play in mud!

But not Ralph Warthog.

Ralph had a secret that nobody knew.

And that secret was that he worried every day...

...and every night.

"What if my tusks never grow?

What if I'm not as tough as my sister?

...Or as warty as Dad?

What if I'm not as gruff as Grandpa?"

WHAT IF?

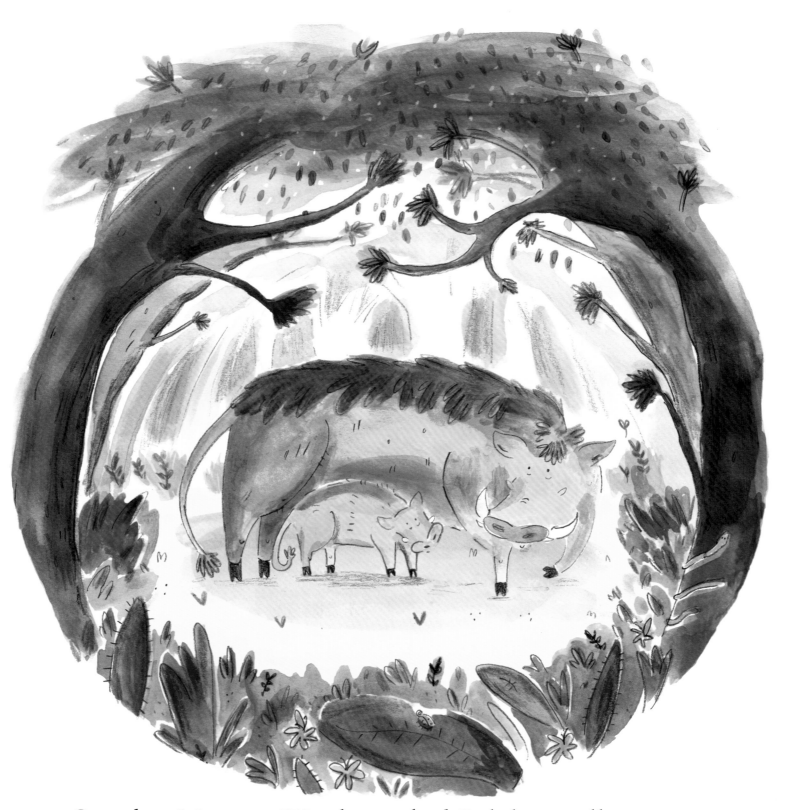

One day, Mummy Warthog asked Ralph to collect some berries from the other side of the watering hole.

"But I don't think I can do it alone," whimpered Ralph. "I believe you can be brave," said Mummy Warthog.

"I CAN be BRAVE!"
(Although he didn't believe it.)

But the worries still came...

"What if there are snakes?"

"What if there are waterfalls?"

"What if there are snakes IN waterfalls?"

Ralph's worries were so big he froze with fear.
"Why are you crying?" asked the hedgehog.

"I'm so worried all the time," sobbed Ralph. "Worries?"
said the hedgehog. "I know a thing or two about worries!"

"When I get worried, I curl into a ball," he said.

"But then I huff... and I puff...

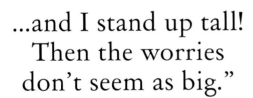
...and I stand up tall!
Then the worries
don't seem as big."

"Look at all these animals. Every single one has their own fears and worries."

"I bet you didn't know that lions are scared of thunderstorms.

Or that the ground squirrel is so nervous about winter, she gathers far too many nuts!

The baboon is terrified of mice.

And even Mr. Frog worries he can't jump as high as his froggy friends!"

Ralph was very relieved to
hear that he wasn't the only
one to worry.

"But how do they solve
their worries?" asked Ralph.

"Well," said the hedgehog, "keeping your worries a secret
only makes you feel worse. So, they talk to their friends,
who help them get through it!"

"Excuse me, could you possibly help me gather some berries for my family?" Ralph asked the animals.

And so they did! Ralph's new friends helped him find his way home through the watering hole.

Mummy Warthog was very pleased to see Ralph's big stash of fruits for the whole family.

"I knew you could be brave!" She said, smiling.

Ralph realised the best way to solve a worry was to be brave and to ask for help...

...or at least talk about it
over a huge feast.

And he always remembered to stand up tall.

Starfish Bay® Children's Books
An imprint of Starfish Bay Publishing
www.starfishbaypublishing.com

THE WORRY WARTHOG

© Lucy Pickett, 2020
ISBN 978-1-76036-066-5
First Published 2020
Printed in China

for my Mum.x